Disney · PIXA

Lots to Discover

PIXAR1256473

Code is valid for your Disney•Pixar ebook and
may be redeemed through the Disney Story Central app
on the App Store. Content subject to availability.
Parent permission required.
Code expires on December 31, 2019.

PaRragon
Bath · New York · Cologne · Melbourne · Delhi
Hong Kong · Shenzhen · Singapore

This edition published by Parragon Books Ltd in 2016 and distributed by

Parragon Inc.
440 Park Avenue South, 13th Floor
New York, NY 10016
www.parragon.com

ISBN: 978-1-4748-3762-0

Printed in US

One day, the Andersens welcomed a baby girl to their family. They named her Riley.

Riley grew up in Minnesota. She made many happy memories there—including learning to play hockey!

All of Riley's core memories were stored in Headquarters,
a place inside her head. Her Emotions lived there, too.
Joy smiled all the time.

Sadness was usually frowning—or crying.

Fear was afraid of everything! Would his tea
burn his tongue? And what was that noise?

That noise might have been Anger blowing his top: what do you mean Riley can't have dessert until she eats her broccoli?!

Disgust believed her high standards for food
and other things kept Riley safe from harm.

Joy was Riley's strongest Emotion, but Joy was always fighting Sadness for control of Headquarters.

When Riley was 11, her family moved to San Francisco.
"You are the best, sweetie," said Riley's mom.
She knew the move was a huge change.

Riley's Emotions were not sure how to feel.

Joy used pep talks and group hugs
to try to get everyone to be happy.

On Riley's first day of school, Joy woke up Headquarters with a lively song!

Riley left the house smiling and feeling ready.

But when her new teacher asked her to talk about Minnesota, Riley suddenly got sad remembering everything she'd left behind.

Oh no! A new, blue, sad core memory
arrived in Headquarters.

Joy tried to get rid of it,
but instead she, Sadness, and
all of Riley's core memories got
sucked out of Headquarters!

The other Emotions had no idea
what to do without Joy and Sadness!

Mom and Dad noticed that Riley
wasn't her usual happy self at dinner.

Meanwhile, Joy was holding tightly to Riley's core memories and trying to figure out how to get back to Headquarters.

Sadness was not convinced they'd ever find
their way back, but Joy refused to give up!

Even so, it was hard for even Joy
to deal with all of Sadness's tears.

Joy and Sadness found the
Train of Thought. They decided
to ride it back to Headquarters!

Inside Headquarters, Fear tried to find new core memories. The Emotions knew that Riley's core memories powered her Islands of Personality and made Riley who she was.

Things weren't going well for Riley. She missed
a goal because Hockey Island wasn't working.

Anger decided that going back to Minnesota
would make everything better. He plugged
his bright idea bulb into the console.

So Riley decided to run away
and go back to Minnesota.

Because Riley stole her mom's credit card to buy her bus ticket, Honesty Island crumbled. It derailed the Train of Thought!

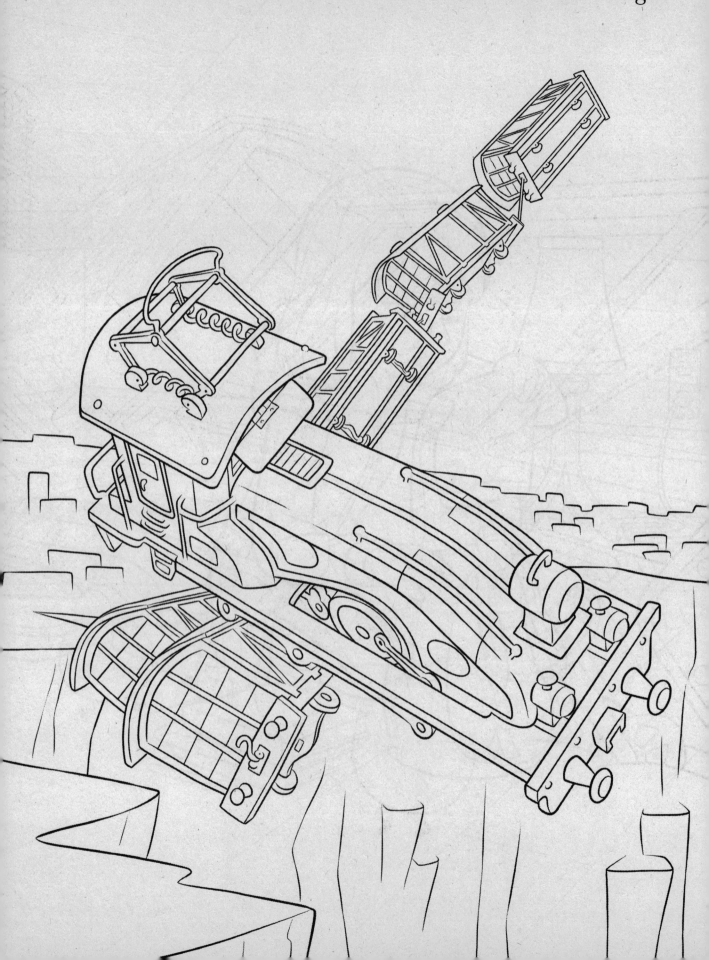

Mind Workers had to rescue Joy
and Sadness from the train wreck.

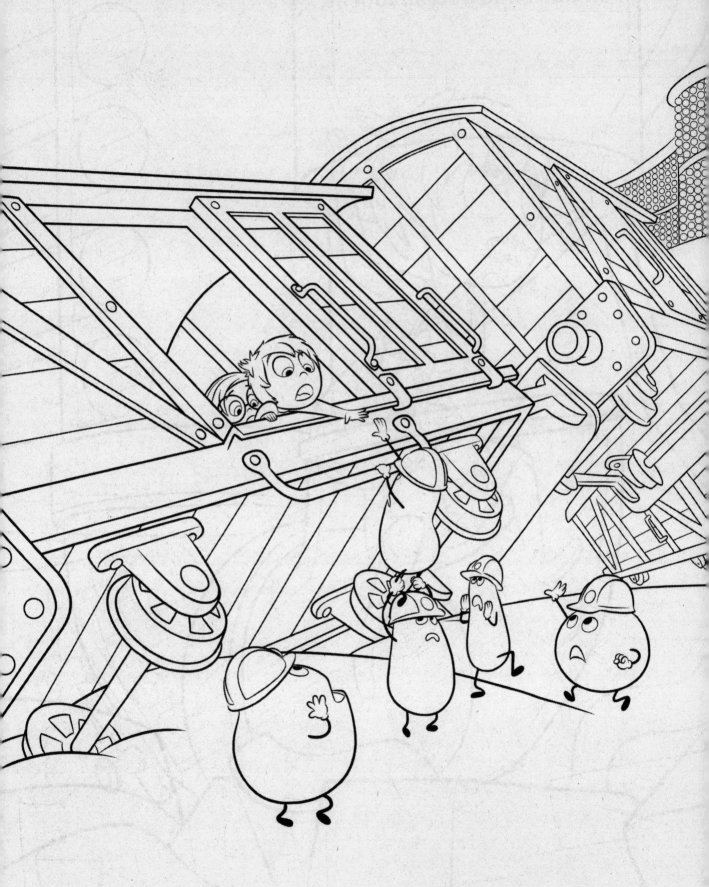

Determined to get back to Headquarters, Joy climbed into a recall tube.

But it failed and
instead deposited her
in the Memory Dump!

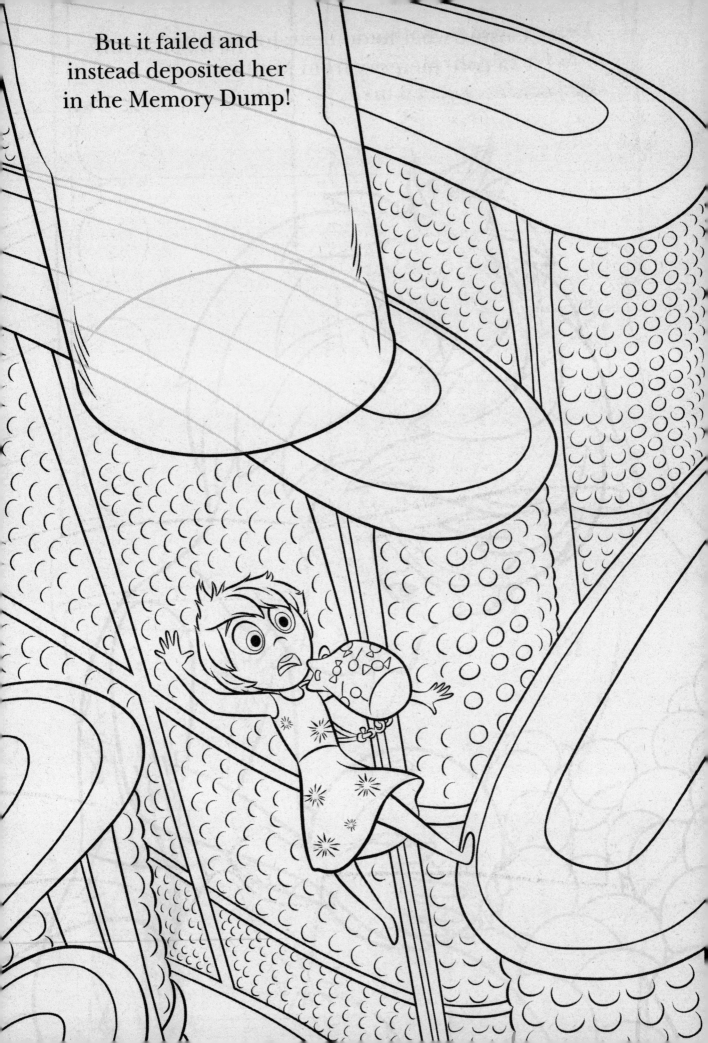

Unsure what to do next, Joy watched
a core memory from Minnesota.

It was the time Riley's teammates cheered her up after she missed a key shot. If Riley hadn't been sad, she couldn't have become happy again. Joy realized she needed Sadness!

Back in Headquarters, Anger tried to get his bright idea bulb out of the console. But it was stuck tight!

Riley boarded the bus to Minnesota.

Sadness, meanwhile, decided Riley was better off without her, and she started to float away.

Joy couldn't let Sadness go! She climbed a stack
of Imaginary Boyfriends to get to Sadness.

The two Emotions finally made
it back to Headquarters. Hooray!

Sadness quickly took control of the console.
She managed to pull out Anger's bright idea bulb!

Joy handed a happy yellow core memory
to Sadness so it could turn blue.

Riley got off the bus and ran all the way home. She cried and told her parents how much she missed Minnesota. They missed it, too!

Talking about her sad feelings helped Riley become happy again. Joy and Sadness were a great team!

With all her Emotions working together, Riley started to like San Francisco—and her new hockey team!

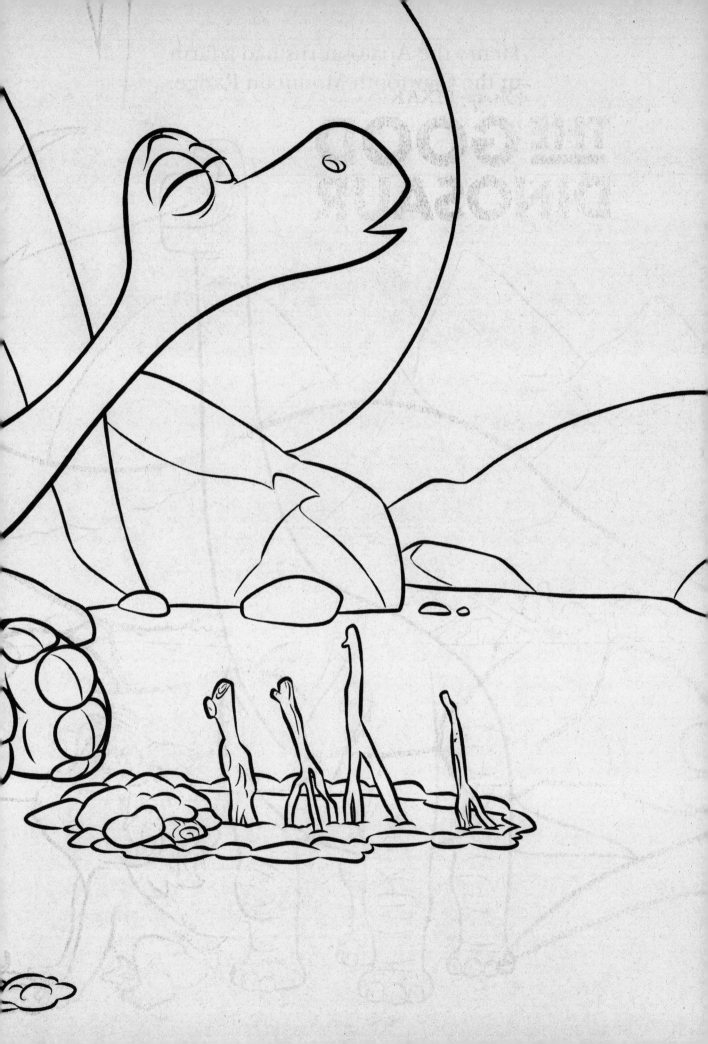

Henry the Apatosaurus had a farm
in the Clawtooth Mountain Range.

His loving wife, Ida, worked by his side.

Together they waited for their last egg to hatch.

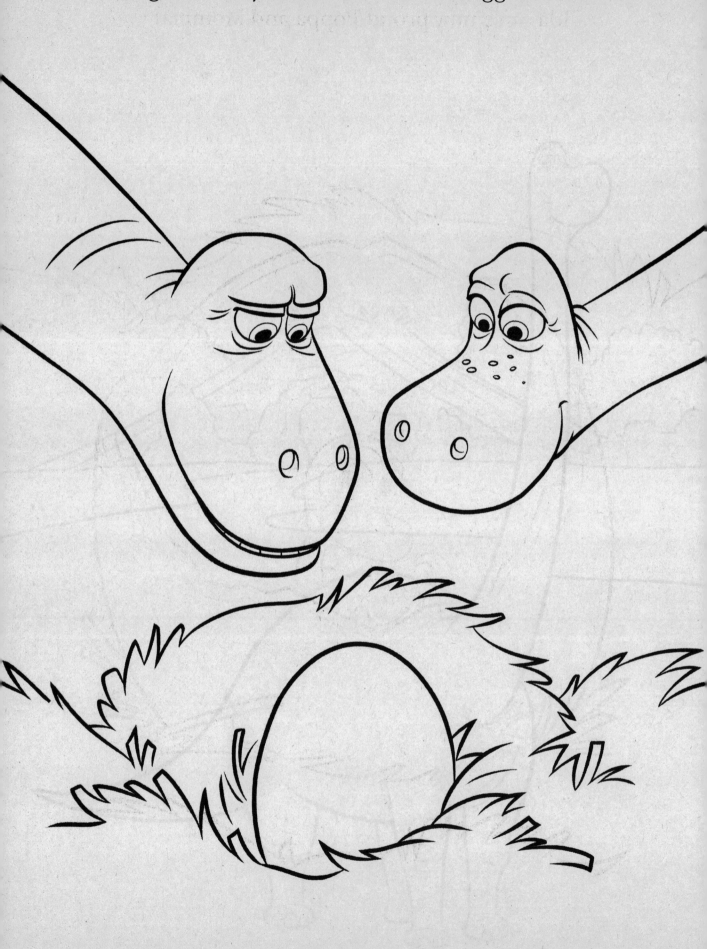

Crack! There was baby Arlo! Henry and
Ida were now proud Poppa and Momma!

Buck was the strongest of the dino babies.

Libby was the bravest and most playful.

Arlo was the smallest of the three.

By the time they were 11, Buck and Libby
were ready to help out on the farm.

Arlo helped, too. His job was to feed the farm's animals.

But sometimes they scared him!

Arlo was scared of a lot of things, including fireflies.

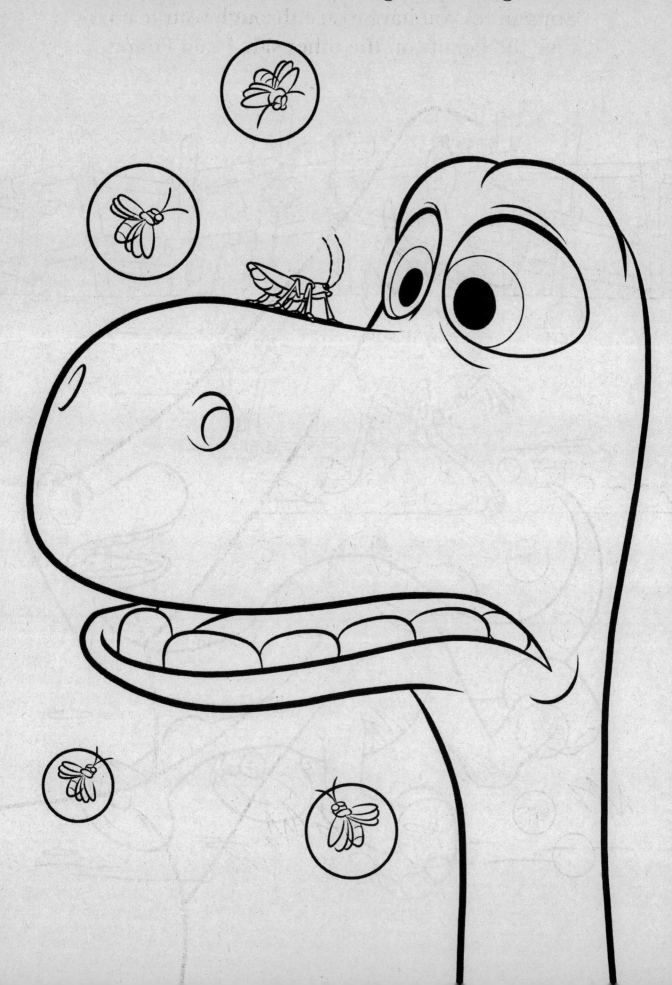

That is, until Poppa showed him that fireflies light up.
"Sometimes you have to see through your fears to
see the beauty on the other side," said Poppa.

When Poppa died, Arlo was determined
to help Momma even more on the farm.

Arlo discovered a critter stealing their corn!

. . . and fell in the river trying to get rid of it!

The current carried Arlo far away, but he knew
he could get home by following the river.

As he walked, Arlo became hungry.
He climbed on some rocks to
reach a few berries.

But the rocks were not steady, and Arlo came crashing down.
His leg became trapped under a giant rock!

Arlo had no choice but to sleep through the night.
He woke to discover that his leg had been freed!
Then he noticed the critter's footprints.

Arlo began walking toward home again, but he had to stop and take shelter when it began to rain.

The critter came back and brought food for Arlo.

Arlo followed the critter to a tree with berries.

The critter clearly liked being around Arlo!
And Arlo liked him, too.

Arlo continued his
journey home, and the
critter came with him.
The two walked up the
side of a mountain.

At the top, they found a giant hissing lizard. It headed straight for Arlo! The critter jumped in and scared off the snake.

A Styracosaurus named Forrest Woodbush saw the critter
protecting Arlo. He wanted the critter for himself.

Forrest challenged Arlo to a contest: whoever called out
a name that the critter responded to would keep him.
Arlo yelled "Spot" and the critter ran to him!

That night, Arlo showed Spot the magic of fireflies. It made him think of Poppa and how much he missed his family.

"Family," said Arlo. He and Spot used sticks to tell each other about their families. Spot was the only one left in his.

The next day, it began to storm.
The thunder and lightning terrified Arlo!

He ran and hid in an old tree.

After the storm, Arlo asked a Pterodactyl named
Thunderclap to help him find the river.

But the Pterodactyls were more interested in making
a meal out of Spot than helping. So Arlo ran away
as fast as he could, with Spot clinging to his back!

Arlo and Spot ran straight into Nash
and Ramsey, two roaring T. rexes!

Nash and Ramsey liked Arlo and Spot,
so they scared off the Pterodactyls.

Arlo and Spot offered to help Nash, Ramsey,
and their dad, Butch, find their herd of longhorns,
which had been stolen by rustlers.

Spot bit Arlo to make him scream loudly
enough to bring the rustlers out of hiding.

It worked! The Raptor rustlers
appeared, claws out, ready to rumble.

With Butch leading the fight, the T. rexes,
Arlo, and Spot defeated the Raptors.

That night, the T. rexes, Arlo, and Spot gathered around the campfire and Nash played his bug harmonica.

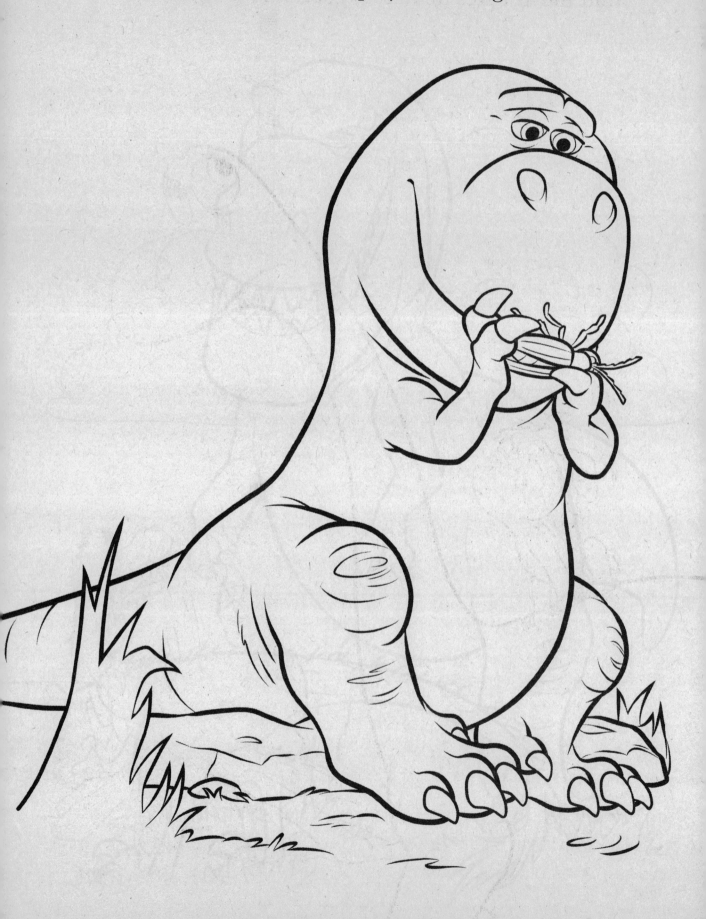

The first snow of the year began to fall, and Arlo told the T. rexes he had to get home to Momma.

The next morning, Arlo spied Clawtooth Mountain.
Now he knew which way to go!

Arlo watched Spot look intently at something in the distance. What was it?

Before he could find out, the Pterodactyls reappeared!

Thunderclap snatched Spot and put him in a tree trunk.

Arlo fought off the Pterodactyls and saved Spot,
only to find floodwaters heading their way!

The two got swept over a waterfall!

Spot and Arlo made it to the riverbank, safe and sound.

The next day, on their way up Clawtooth Mountain, Arlo and Spot met a human family that wanted to adopt Spot.

Arlo and Spot had become great friends, but Spot
belonged with humans. He and Arlo hugged goodbye.

Arlo finally made it home! He realized he had left home scared of everything and had returned able to handle anything—just like Poppa.

Lightning McQueen arrived for the
Piston Cup championship race. Winning was
the most important thing in the world to him.

Out on the track, Lightning wove his way through the other cars easily, showing off his racing skills.

But when Chick caused a crash, Lightning
blew a tire trying to avoid it. He lost his lead!

The race ended in a three-way tie between
Lightning, the King, and Chick.

Lightning bragged to reporters that he would
win the tie-breaking race in Los Angeles.

Lightning zoomed eagerly back onto
Mack, his truck, for the journey.

That night, on the road, other cars jostled a sleepy Mack.

The back of the trailer opened,
and Lightning slid down the
ramp into oncoming traffic!

Lightning drove at top speed, searching for Mack.
He destroyed miles of road in a town called Radiator Springs
and wound up tangled in telephone wires!

The next morning, Lightning woke up
to find he was impounded.

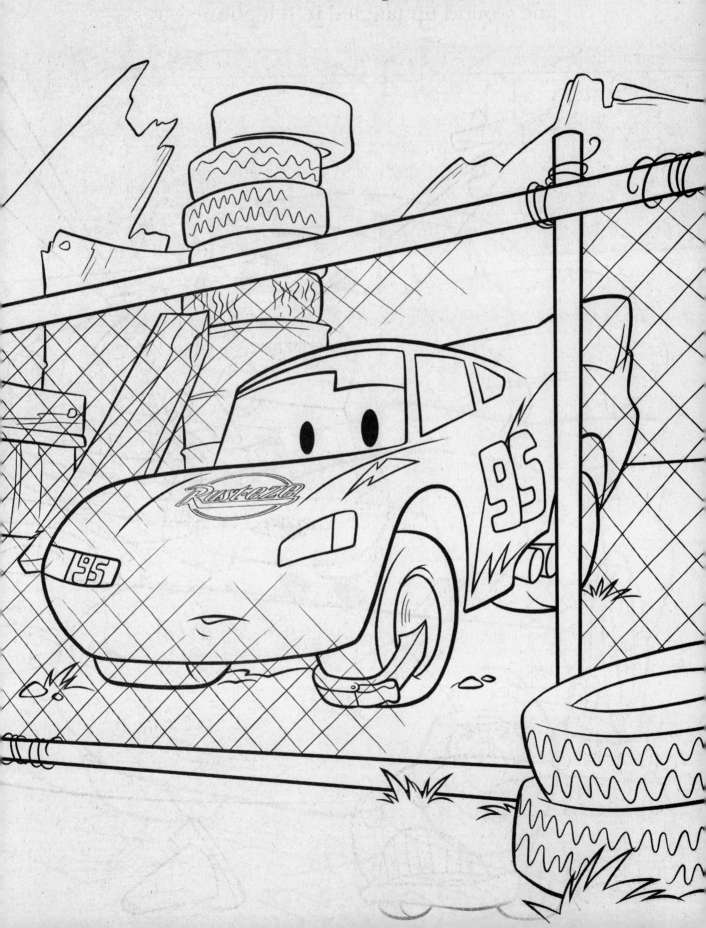

Doc Hudson, the judge of Radiator Springs,
decided to release Lightning.

Then he ordered Lightning to work with
Bessie to repair the roads he had destroyed.

Lightning met everyone in Radiator Springs, including Sally, a beautiful sports car, who was the town's lawyer.

Mater was a rusty tow truck with a big heart.

Luigi ran the local tire shop, Luigi's Casa Della Tires.

Guido was Luigi's assistant and best friend.

Fillmore brewed organic fuel.

Ramone owned the town's custom body and paint shop.

After Lightning did a terrible job fixing the road,
Doc challenged him to a race.

Doc told Lightning he could leave Radiator Springs if he won.
If Lightning lost, he had to stay and fix the road properly.

Lightning thought it would be easy to beat Doc, but he wound up taking a turn too fast and going off the road.

Lightning discovered that Doc had won the Piston Cup three times before being involved in a terrible crash. By the time Doc recovered, the racing world had forgotten him.

Sally took Lightning on a drive up the mountain.

She stopped to show him an amazing view of Radiator Springs
and told him that it had once been a busy place—until
a big highway was built that bypassed the town.

The next morning everyone was excited
to see that the road had been fixed.

Lightning had done it! Sally had made him understand how important Radiator Springs was to everyone who lived there. Lightning had even gotten a respray from Ramone.

All of a sudden, Mack rolled into town. He had
been searching for Lightning everywhere.

Lightning had to get to Los Angeles for the race.
He tried to say goodbye to Sally, but he
couldn't find the right words.

At the Speedway in Los Angeles, the race began, but Lightning couldn't concentrate. All he could think about was Radiator Springs.

Lightning could not believe his eyes: Doc had brought him a pit crew from Radiator Springs!

Lightning gained the lead, but then Chick clipped the King, who was racing his last race. Lightning slammed on his brakes and Chick sped across the finish line.

As the crowd roared, Lightning pushed the King across the finish line. He had learned that some things were more important than winning.

Marlin was a worrier. The thing he worried about most was keeping his son, Nemo, safe.

Marlin was very worried the day Mr. Ray announced that he was taking Nemo's class on a field trip to the coral reef!

Nemo went to the coral reef Drop-off with some of his friends.

To show how brave he was, Nemo swam out
to a boat. As Marlin and the others watched,
Nemo was captured by a diver!

Marlin was frantic. He asked everyone if they had seen the "fish-nappers," but no one answered him.

Finally, a fish named Dory offered to help him.

Dory told Marlin to follow her.
She swam faster and faster and
kept looking behind her.

Then Dory whipped around and asked Marlin why he was following her! Dory had some short-term memory problems.

Dory and Marlin met a shark named Bruce.
He invited them to a party with sharks
who had pledged to stop eating fish.

At the party, Bruce suddenly decided that he did want to eat Dory and Marlin—but they managed to escape.

Dory and Marlin found a mask from one
of the divers who had captured Nemo.

With the help of an anglerfish, they were able
to see the words on the mask. Dory read out loud,
"P. Sherman, 42 Wallaby Way, Sydney."

Nemo was at 42 Wallaby Way—stuck in
a fish tank in a dentist's office!

And he was not alone. The tank was filled with an assortment of odd fish.

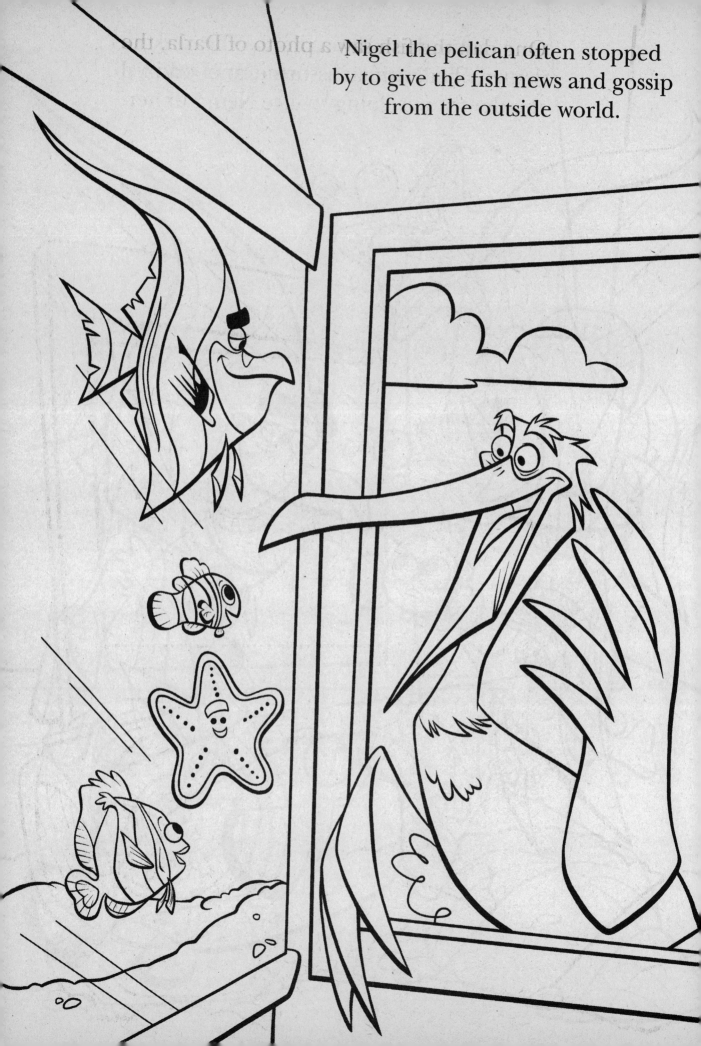

Nigel the pelican often stopped
by to give the fish news and gossip
from the outside world.

One day, the fish saw a photo of Darla, the
dentist's badly behaved niece, and realized
the dentist was going to give Nemo to her.

Meanwhile, in the ocean, Dory got directions
to the dentist's office from a group of moonfish.

Marlin swam off before he heard them tell Dory that they should swim through and not over the big trench.

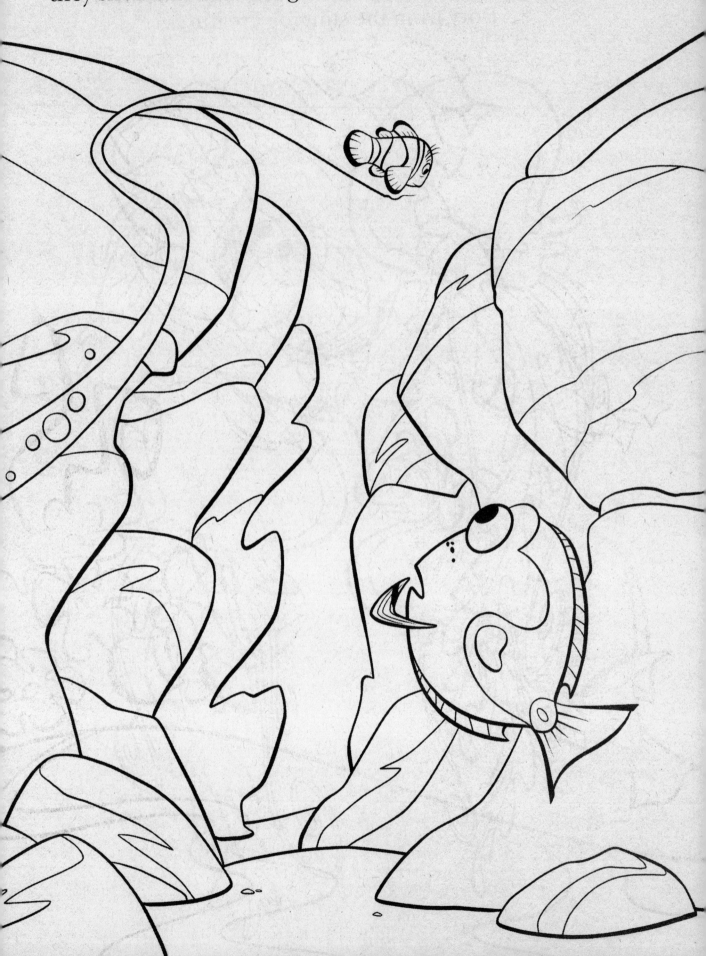

At the top of the big trench, they were surrounded
by a large group of jellyfish. Marlin had to rescue
Dory from the stinging creatures.

Dory and Marlin hitched rides with some very relaxed sea turtles. The sea turtles quickly spread the word about Nemo to everyone in the ocean.

After they left the sea turtles, Dory and Marlin asked a whale for help, but they wound up inside her mouth!

Suddenly, the whale stopped and blew Dory and Marlin out of her spout and into Sydney Harbor—she had helped them get to Nemo!

The pelicans in Sydney Harbor were all talking about Marlin and his heroic journey to find his son.

Nigel flew to the dentist's office
and told Nemo about his father.
Nemo was so proud!

Later, the dentist arrived. He scooped
Nemo up and put him in a plastic bag.

There was Darla! She had come to collect her new fish.

Over on the docks, Nigel recognized Marlin and Dory and offered to take them to Nemo.

Nigel, Marlin, and Dory arrived at the dentist's office.

They saw Nemo upside down in the bag.
They didn't know he was only pretending to
be dead so he wouldn't have to go with Darla.

Gill jumped out of the tank and flipped Nemo down
the drain so that he would wind up in the harbor!

Marlin and Dory were back in the harbor. Marlin was numb with sadness. He said goodbye to Dory and swam off.

Dory saw Nemo and actually remembered she knew his father. She reunited them, and Marlin—for at least that moment—wasn't worried about one little thing!

It was another night of work at Monsters, Inc.
Sulley, the company's number one Scarer,
waved hello to his coworkers.

Mike was Sulley's assistant. He waved, too.

In the locker room, Mike had an unpleasant encounter with Randall, the number two Scarer, who would do anything to beat Sulley.

Then scary Roz reminded Mike that he still
owed her his paperwork. Mike hated paperwork.

So on his way to the Scare Floor, Mike paused
by the reception desk to see his girlfriend, Celia.
She could always cheer him up!

It was time to get started!
The Scarers walked onto the Scare Floor.

Sulley was ready to go behind as many doors on the Scare Floor as he could. The doors led to children's bedrooms, and Sulley's job was to scare the children.

Mike then collected their screams in canisters,
because those screams were used to power everything
in Monstropolis. Sulley and Mike were a great team!

Monsters were checked to make sure they didn't
accidentally bring anything back from the human world.
Children and their things were considered toxic!

The CDA—Child Detection Agency—
swarmed in to deal with any problems.

Sulley was always very careful. Mr. Waternoose,
Monsters, Inc.'s president, was proud of his top Scarer!

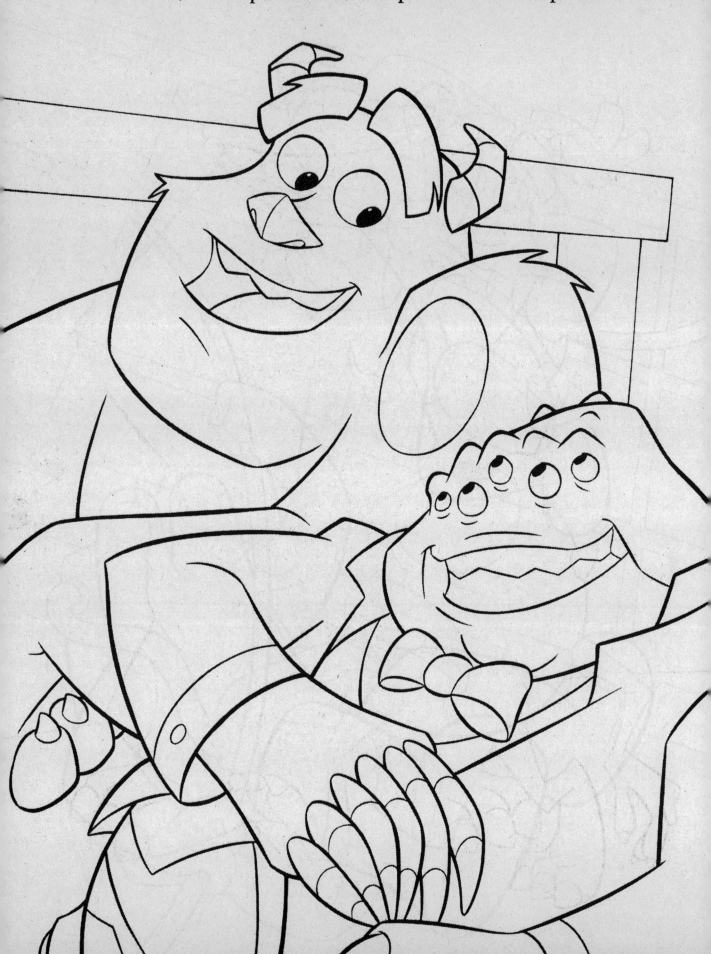

At the end of the night, Sulley told Mike he'd stay behind and do the paperwork so that Mike could take Celia on a date.

When Sulley walked onto the Scare Floor, he found one active door still there. Puzzled, he opened it to take a look inside.

Oh no! Sulley accidentally let a child onto the Scare Floor!

Sulley tried to get the little girl back
through the door and into her room.

But it didn't work! Sulley put the little girl in a duffel bag and then hid from Randall, who saw the door and returned it to the vault.

Sulley needed Mike's help to figure out
what to do now that the door was gone,
so he went to the restaurant where
Mike and Celia were having dinner.

Sulley tried to quietly tell Mike that there was a child in the duffel bag.

But the child got out! Everyone saw her and panicked!

Sulley scooped up the child, and he and Mike ran off while the CDA arrived and blew up the contaminated restaurant.

They took the child to their apartment,
where they watched her from a safe distance.

Sulley thought the child might not be dangerous
after all, but he and Mike still needed to figure
out how to get her safely back home.

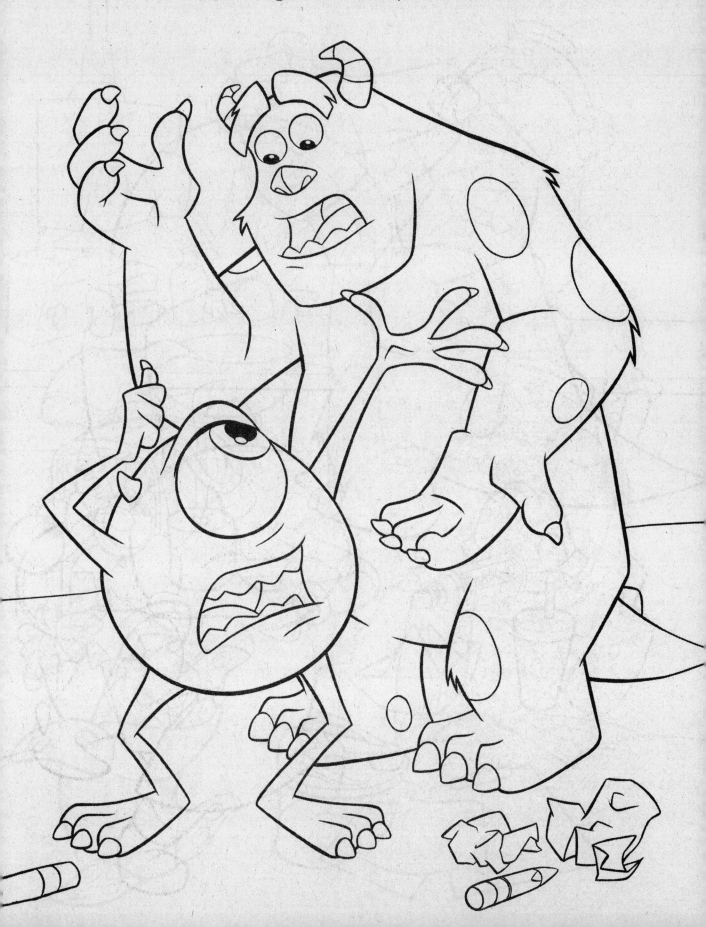

The next day, they took the little
girl to work disguised as a monster.

Mike tried but couldn't get the card key for the child's door.

Mike and Sulley hid with the child when
Randall came into the locker room.

Mike heard Sulley call the little girl Boo. He got really angry. "Sulley," he cried. "You're not supposed to name it!"

Suddenly, Mike and Sulley noticed Boo was gone!
They began a frantic search for her.

Boo had wandered off and joined
the Monsters, Inc. daycare group!

Sulley was so relieved, he swept Boo up and gave her a giant hug.

Then they went to the Scare Floor, where a door
that looked like Boo's was waiting at Sulley's station.

Sulley hesitated. Randall had put the door there as an offer to help when he realized that Sulley and Mike had Boo. But Sulley did not trust Randall.

Sulley was right. Randall tried to capture Boo,
but Sulley and Mike managed to escape with her.

Sulley wanted to ask Waternoose for help, but his boss made him roar first to teach the new recruits. Boo was terrified!

To Sulley's horror, he found out that Waternoose
and Randall were working together!

Then Sulley and Mike were thrown through a door into a snowy, frozen place. They were exiled from Monstropolis!

Thwack! Suddenly, Sulley got hit with a snowball.

It was the Abominable Snowman! Just when all hope seemed lost, he told Mike and Sulley about a nearby town.

Sulley and Mike hurried to the town. They ran through a child's door and back onto the Scare Floor!

Sulley and Mike grabbed Boo, and
the three went on the run again!

Waternoose and Randall were furious—they wanted
to keep Boo in Monstropolis to harness her screams.
They planned to kidnap as many children as possible.

Celia helped Mike and Sulley get away: she made a fake
announcement that Randall had broken the scare record.

The workers surrounded Randall to congratulate him.

While Randall was busy, Sulley and Mike ran
to the conveyor belt to look for Boo's door.

But before long, Randall was on their trail again!

Mike and Sulley discovered that Boo's laughter had more power than her screams, so Mike made her laugh to open the doors.

Sulley and Mike pushed Randall through an open door—he disappeared into the human world and was never heard from again.

But their troubles were not over yet. Waternoose and
the CDA made them come down to the Scare Floor.

Mike told everyone Waternoose's plan
to bring more kids to Monstropolis.

The CDA closed in on Waternoose and dragged him away.

Finally, Mike found Boo's door!

Sulley was sad to say goodbye, but he was happy to get Boo home safely.

Thanks to Boo, Monsters, Inc. would now harness kids' laughter instead of their screams!

When Andy was a little boy, he
played with his toys all the time.

But now he was 17, and he had no time for them.

"Andy's going to college soon," Woody told the other toys. "But he's going to take care of us. I guarantee it."

Andy put all of his toys in a trash bag—except for Woody.
He was going to store them in the attic.

But there was a terrible misunderstanding.
Mom found the trash bag in the
hall and thought Andy wanted
to throw it away!

Woody tried to save his friends before the garbage truck
swallowed them up, not realizing they had already broken free.

The toys made it to the garage. Thinking that Andy had planned to throw them away, they decided to get in the donation box Mom had in the car.

They didn't believe Woody when he climbed into
the box and tried to explain that it was all a mistake.
The toys let Mom take them to the Sunnyside Daycare.

Lotso, Sunnyside's head toy, greeted them.

They met Twitch, Chunk, and Sparks, too.

Stretch introduced herself to Slinky and Hamm.

A jack-in-the-box shook hands with Jessie.

"Oooh! The Claw!" the Aliens said excitedly.

Rex roared with delight at finding some new dino pals.

"It's nice here," said Woody. "But we need to go home now." None of the other toys wanted to leave.

So Woody left by himself. He used an old
kite to get from the roof to the ground.

But a strong gust of wind caused Woody to wind up
hanging from his pull-string on a tree branch.
He had lost his cowboy hat.

A little girl named Bonnie, who went to
Sunnyside, found Woody and took him home.

In Bonnie's room, Woody met Mr. Pricklepants.

He met the easygoing Buttercup.

Trixie the Triceratops was happy to meet Woody.

Dolly and the Three-Peas-in-a-Pod also greeted Woody. Bonnie had very nice toys, but all Woody wanted to do was leave.

Meanwhile, back at Sunnyside, Lotso forced Andy's toys to be in the Caterpillar Room with the youngest kids, who played rough!

One toddler banged Buzz against another toy again and again.

Then, Buzz was tossed onto the windowsill that separated the Caterpillar Room from the Butterfly Room, where the older kids played. Things looked much gentler in there.

That night, Buzz
went looking for Lotso.
He wanted to know why they
were stuck in the dangerous
Caterpillar Room. He saw
some toys climbing to the
top of a vending machine.

Buzz overheard them saying that someone had to deal with the rough toddlers and that it was going to be the new toys!

Before he could warn his friends,
Buzz was discovered and tied to a chair!

To keep Buzz quiet, Lotso read Buzz's toy manual
and returned him to his original factory settings.

Now Buzz was working for Lotso!

When Andy's toys complained and said they needed to go home, Lotso had Buzz capture them.

"Buzz, we're
your friends!"
said Jessie.
But Buzz no
longer knew that.

Lotso's gang quickly locked up all of
Andy's toys. He told Buzz to guard them.

Meanwhile, Woody used Bonnie's computer and
discovered that Andy's house was just around the corner!

Then Woody found out from Bonnie's toys what really went on at Sunnyside. Instead of going home, he climbed into Bonnie's backpack—he was going to rescue his friends!

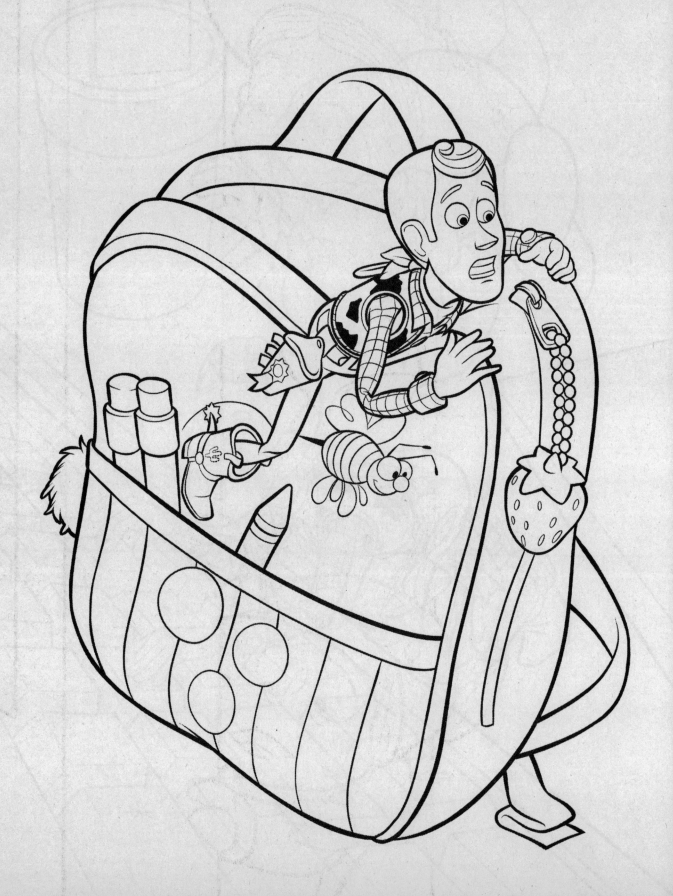

Andy's toys worked together to get out of their cells.

Then they managed to capture Buzz.

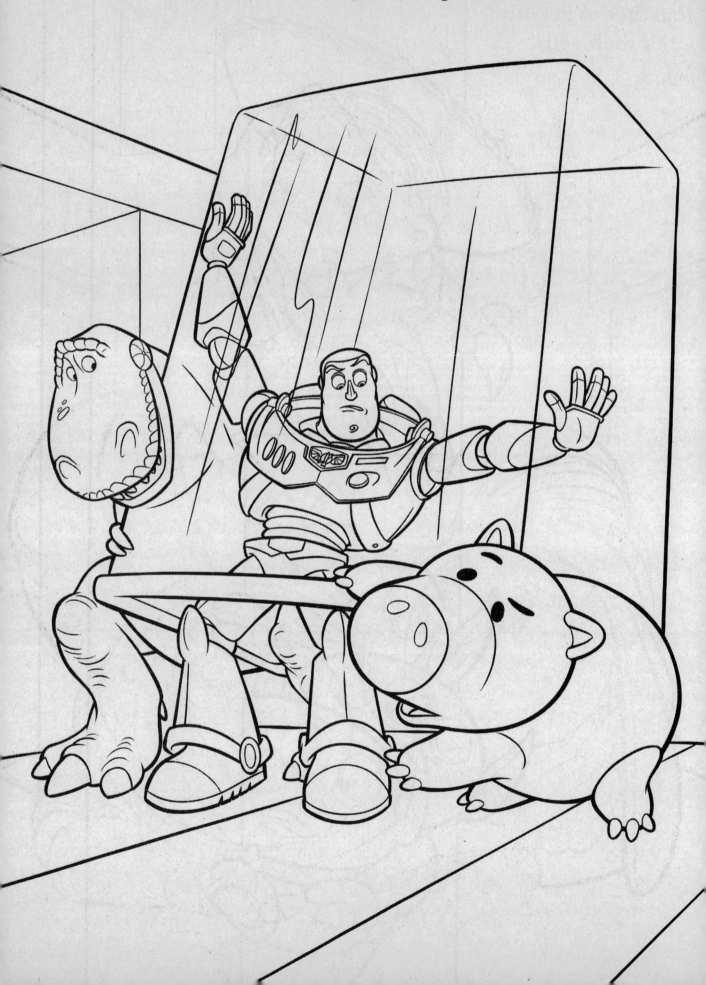

Rex pressed Buzz's reset button.

But something went wrong—now Buzz was speaking Spanish!

Suddenly, Woody arrived. Andy's toys were overjoyed to see him!

Andy's toys made it out of the building and slid down the trash chute to get to freedom!

But Lotso and his gang were waiting for them! All that stood between the two groups was an open dumpster.

Woody pulled out a pendant that had belonged
to Big Baby, one of Lotso's gang. It reminded
Big Baby that he had once been loved very much.

Lotso angrily crushed the pendant. Big Baby reacted by throwing Lotso into the dumpster and slamming the lid!

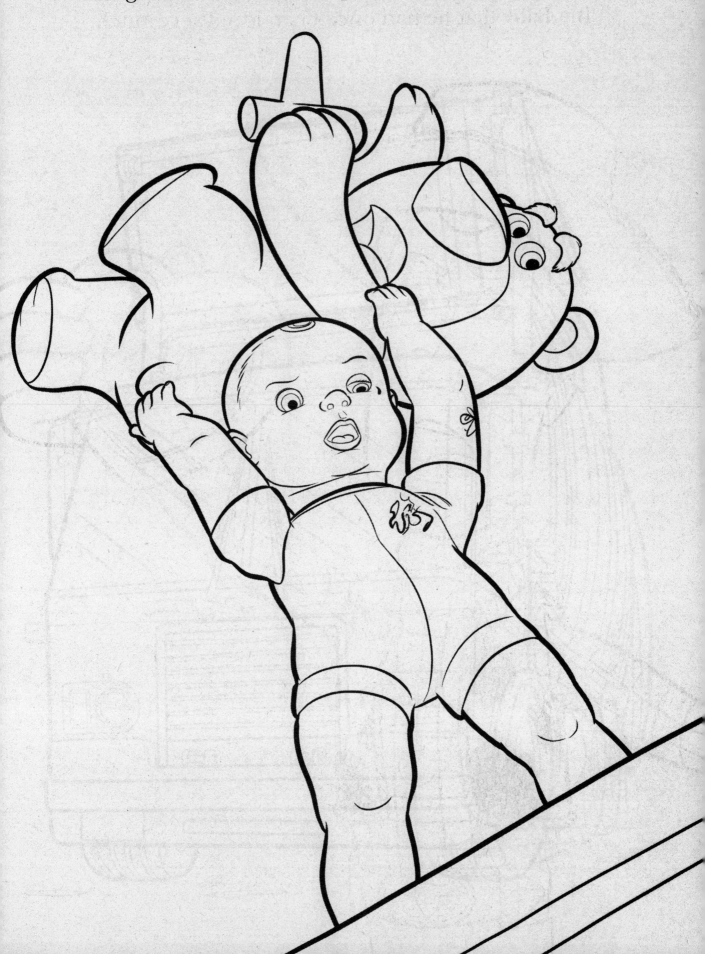

Just then, a garbage truck arrived and lifted the dumpster,
with Andy's toys clinging to the lid, into the truck.

Garbage poured down on them. One piece of trash knocked into Buzz and he was his normal self again!

At the landfill, the truck dumped its entire load, including the toys. The Aliens ran off toward a huge crane. "The Claw!" they cried.

Woody tried to run after them, but he and some of the others got scooped up and pushed by a bulldozer.

The toys found themselves on a conveyor
belt headed toward the incinerator!

Woody and the others had helped free Lotso from the trash.
Now Lotso spotted an Emergency Stop Button,
but instead of pushing it, he ran away!

The friends clasped hands,
determined to face their fate together.

Suddenly, the giant crane
plucked up all of Andy's Toys.
The Aliens had saved them!

As for Lotso, a garbage
truck driver found him
and tied him to the
front of his truck.

The toys had to hitch a ride on another garbage truck
to get back to Andy's house before he left for college.

At Andy's house, everyone got a quick bath.

Then they snuck back into the house and into the box marked "Attic." Buzz shook Woody's hand to wish him well at college.

Woody thought for a minute, then quickly
scribbled a note and put it on the Attic box.

The note told Andy to donate the box to a girl named Bonnie.

Andy stopped by Bonnie's house on his way
to college. He introduced Bonnie to all the toys—
including Woody, who had put himself in the box!

Bonnie hugged Woody and promised
to take good care of them all!

Mr. Incredible was the most popular Super alive!

His best friend, Frozone, was the coolest Super on the planet. He could make ice and travel on it.

Mr. Incredible was married to Elastigirl—
no one could stretch like her!

Mr. Incredible was always ready to help anyone in need.

He even kept Buddy, the president
of his fan club, safe from harm.

But then the government made all Supers
give up their Super ways. For the next 15 years,
Mr. Incredible worked in insurance as Bob Parr.

Bob still sometimes forgot he wasn't supposed to do Super things anymore.

Elastigirl, now Helen Parr, still stretched things a bit while taking care of their kids.

On bowling nights, Bob and Frozone, who was now called Lucius, listened to the police radio.

One night, they heard there was a fire in the vicinity. They couldn't help themselves: they put on masks and went to rescue people.

One day, a mysterious woman named Mirage told Bob he had been chosen for a top-secret government mission to stop the destructive Omnidroid 9000 robot.

Bob took the job, but didn't tell Helen. He and
Mirage flew off to the island of Nomanisan.

Shortly after they landed, Mr. Incredible had his first encounter with the Omnidroid.

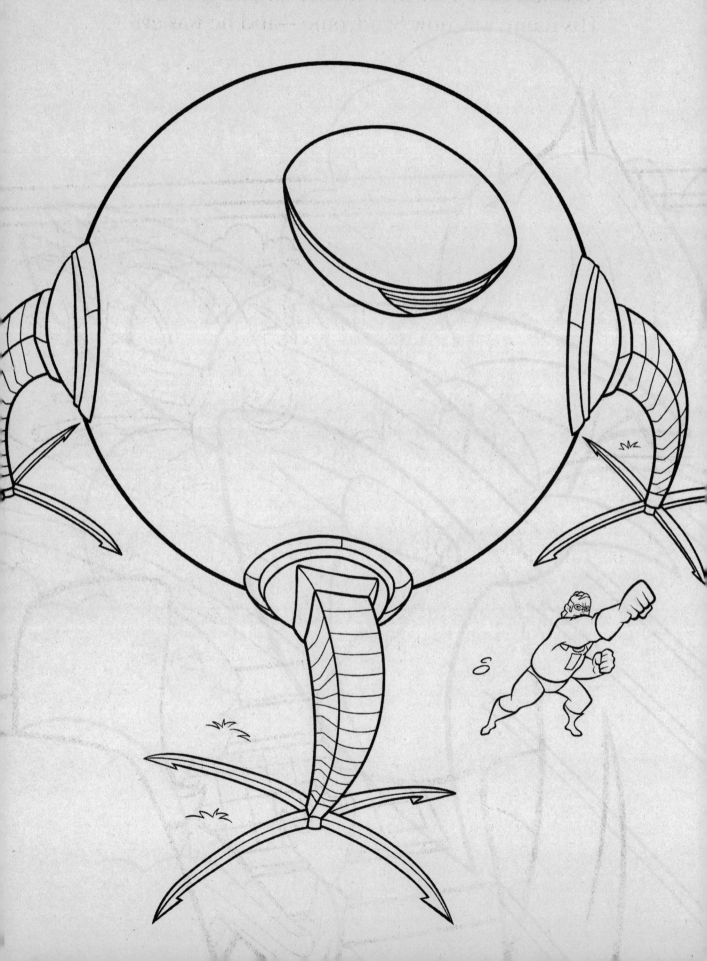

He easily defeated the robot. Mirage and her boss watched. Her boss was Buddy, all grown up. His name was now Syndrome—and he was evil.

Meanwhile, a suspicious Helen visited
famous Super suit designer, Edna.
She learned that her husband was back in
the Super business—with a new Super suit!

Edna gave Helen new Super suits for the whole family and a device that let her track Bob's whereabouts.

Helen found out that Bob was on Nomanisan.
While she got ready to go after him, her oldest
children, Violet and Dash, found their Super suits.

Helen flew off to find Bob.
She had two stowaways on
board—Violet and Dash.

Back on Nomanisan, Mr. Incredible had discovered that Syndrome wanted to destroy him. He managed to sneak into Syndrome's base.

Using his laser vision, Mr. Incredible discovered
the word KRONOS. It was a password!

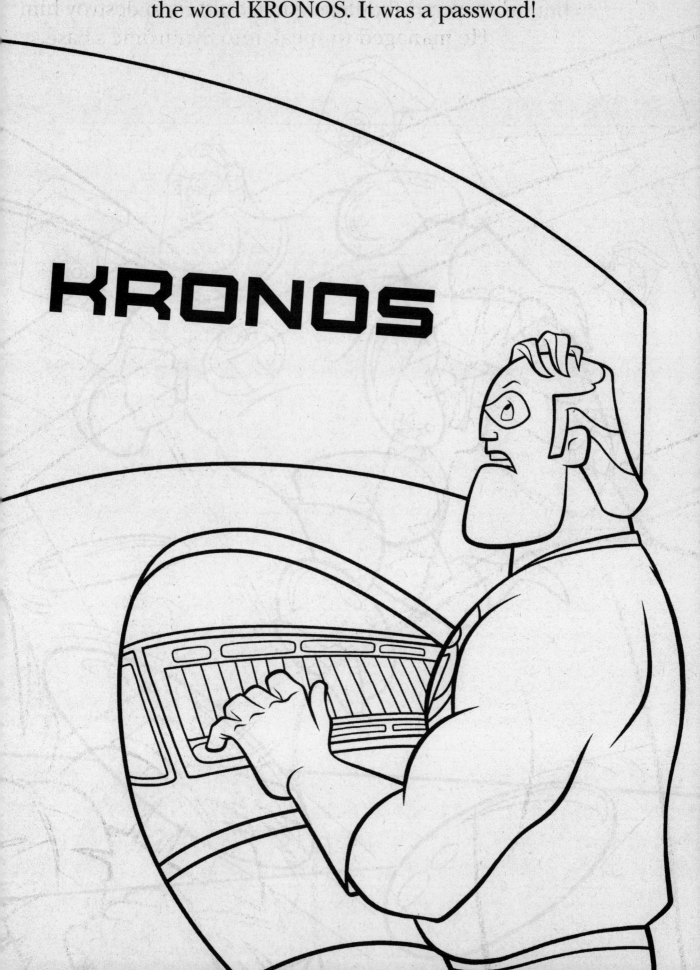

Mr. Incredible learned all of Syndrome's evil plans,
but he was captured before he could escape.

Mr. Incredible watched helplessly as
Syndrome sent missiles to attack Helen's jet.

Helen avoided the missiles and got
everyone safely to the island, where
they suited up to go find Bob.

It was an easy stretch for Elastigirl
to get into Syndrome's headquarters.

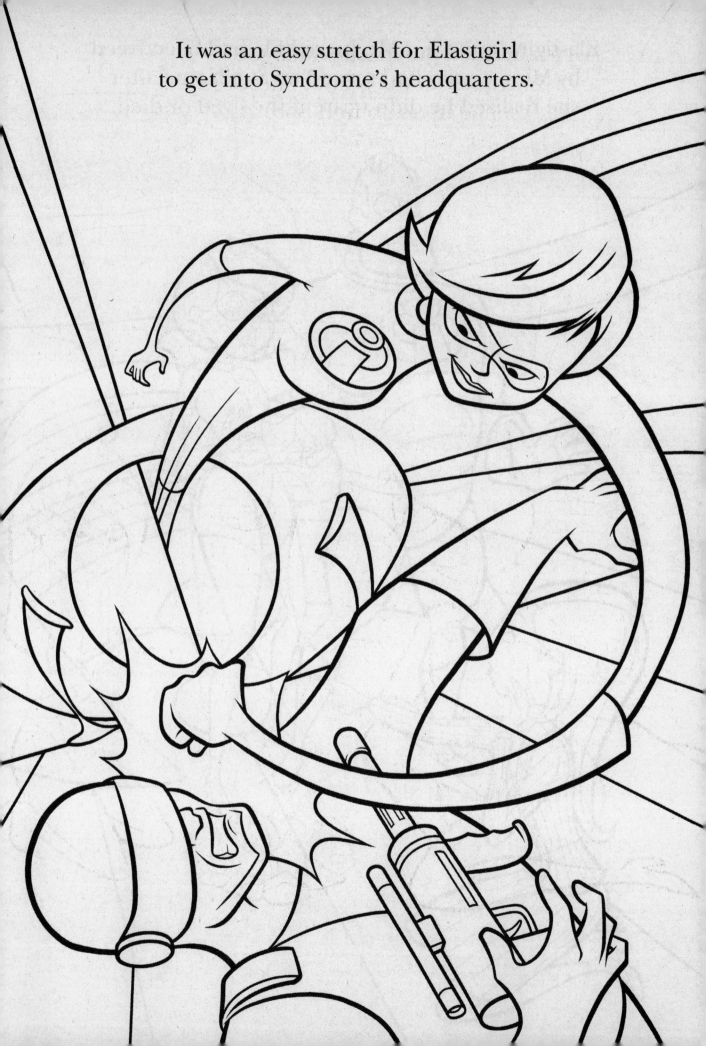

Elastigirl found out Mr. Incredible had been freed by Mirage, who had turned on Syndrome after she realized he didn't care if she lived or died.

Mirage told them that Dash and Violet had set off
Syndrome's alarm. They raced to rescue their kids!

Mr. Incredible and Elastigirl defeated the guards.

CRASH!

Violet and Dash were face-to-face with Syndrome.

Syndrome told the whole family his evil plan: he was sending the Omnidroid to Metroville.

He was the only one who would know how to defeat it—
Syndrome would be declared the world's best Super!

However, once they arrived in Metroville, things did not go as Syndrome planned. The Omnidroid knocked Syndrome out!

Mr. Incredible apologized to Elastigirl for not realizing that his biggest adventure was his family. He told her they were going to stop the Omnidroid as a family!

Mr. Incredible tossed the Omnidroid's remote control to Dash.

Together, the family destroyed the Omnidroid
and then sent it crashing into the ocean.

The Parrs went back to being just another normal family—
but there was something Super about them!